MW00965328

Secret Spies

⭐ Kids Can Read ® Kids Can Read is a registered trademark of Kids Can Press Ltd.

Text © 2000 Adrienne Mason
Illustrations © 2000 Pat Cupples
Revised edition © 2008

All rights reserved. No part of this publication may be reproduced, stored in a retrieval system or transmitted, in any form or by any means, without the prior written permission of Kids Can Press Ltd. or, in case of photocopying or other reprographic copying, a license from The Canadian Copyright Licensing Agency (Access Copyright). For an Access Copyright license, visit www.accesscopyright.ca or call toll free to 1-800-893-5777.

Kids Can Press acknowledges the financial support of the Government of Ontario, through the Ontario Media Development Corporation's Ontario Book Initiative; the Ontario Arts Council; the Canada Council for the Arts; and the Government of Canada, through the BPIDP, for our publishing activity.

Published in Canada by
Kids Can Press Ltd.
29 Birch Avenue
Toronto, ON M4V 1E2

Published in the U.S. by
Kids Can Press Ltd.
2250 Military Road
Tonawanda, NY 14150

www.kidscanpress.com

Adapted by Adrienne Mason from the book *Spy Stuff*.

Edited by David MacDonald
Designed by Kathleen Collett

Printed and bound in Singapore

The paper used to print this book was produced with elemental chlorine-free pulp, harvested from managed sustainable forests.

The hardcover edition of this book is smyth sewn casebound.
The paperback edition of this book is limp sewn with a drawn-on cover.

CM 08 0 9 8 7 6 5 4 3 2 1
CM PA 08 0 9 8 7 6 5 4 3 2 1

Library and Archives Canada Cataloguing in Publication

Mason, Adrienne
    Secret spies / written by Adrienne Mason ; illustrated by Pat Cupples.

Interest age level: Ages 6–7.

ISBN 978-1-55453-276-6 (bound).   ISBN 978-1-55453-277-3 (pbk.)

I. Cupples, Patricia II. Title.

PS8576.A85953S43 2008   jC813'.54   C2007-906551-1

Kids Can Press is a /©ΓUS™ Entertainment company

Secret Spies

Written by Adrienne Mason

Illustrated by Pat Cupples

Kids Can Press

Lu loved to read the comics.

She read them in her cozy chair.

She read them on her bed.

She read them at the breakfast table.

But today, Sophie wanted to play with Lu.

She wanted to do crafts.

Or climb a tree.

Or make lunch.

Lu did not want to play

with her sister, Sophie.

This was Lu's day off.

She did not want to babysit.

She wanted to relax.

Ding dong.

The doorbell rang.

"Who could that be?" asked Lu.

She opened the door.

All she could see was a tuba with legs.

Behind that tuba was Clancy.

Lu and Clancy were best friends.

They were dog detectives, too.

They found lost baseballs,

and stolen ribbons,

and missing mittens,

and sometimes more.

Today they were going to find costumes

for Dress-Up Day at school.

"Let's go look in the attic," said Lu.

"I think I saw an old trunk

with costumes in it."

Lu and Clancy went up to the attic.

"Achoo!" Clancy sneezed.

He brushed a cobweb off his nose.

"This is Aunt Izzy's trunk," said Lu.

She lifted the lid.

There were wigs and costumes,

maps and much more.

Clancy found a map

that said "Top Secret."

Lu found a note written in code.

"Is Aunt Izzy a spy?" asked Lu.

"We are dog detectives," said Clancy.

"Let's find out."

Lu and Clancy decided

to follow Aunt Izzy.

"We can put on costumes so she

will not know who we are," said Lu.

They put on clothes

they found in Aunt Izzy's trunk.

Soon, they looked a lot different —

and a little strange.

"Let's go," said Lu.

"Can I come, too?" said Sophie.

"No," said Clancy.

"This is top secret."

Lu and Clancy put some spy stuff

in a backpack.

They packed a spy camera,

a spy phone,

a secret code book

and their Super Spy Scope.

Then they set off to find Aunt Izzy.

They found her at home.

Lu and Clancy hid

behind a newspaper.

"What is she doing?" asked Clancy.

"She might be waiting for

a secret message," said Lu.

Lu and Clancy waited.

Lu read her secret code book.

Then Aunt Izzy left the room.

Soon she came out the front door.

"Quick! Let's follow her,"

said Clancy.

"Okay, but not too close," said Lu.

Aunt Izzy stopped at the park

to watch a butterfly.

She stopped at the bakery

to buy a donut.

Finally, she went into a shop.

"She is getting a fluff and trim,"

Clancy said.

Lu used her Super Spy Scope

to take a peek.

"Maybe the other dog is a spy, too,"

she said.

Soon the door opened.

A dog came out

in a cloud of perfume and powder.

Sparkly glasses twinkled in the sun.

"She smells different," said Lu.

"But that is Aunt Izzy. Let's go!"

Aunt Izzy stopped to make

a phone call.

Lu listened and talked to Clancy

through the spy phone.

"She is going to meet someone

at the ice-cream stand," said Lu.

Who was she going to meet?

Lu and Clancy followed Aunt Izzy

to the park.

Lu sat on a swing.

"Clancy, you watch Aunt Izzy,"

Lu said.

"I will watch to see

who comes into the park."

"She is going to the ice-cream stand,"

called Clancy.

"Come on, Lu!"

Aunt Izzy bumped into

a dog on skates.

Then she talked to

the ice-cream man.

"Maybe they are

all spies," said Lu.

"Oh, no! Look!" said Clancy.

"Here comes Sophie."

"Duck!" said Lu.

When they looked again,

Sophie was gone.

Aunt Izzy was gone, too.

"Where did Aunty Izzy go?"

asked Lu.

"And who did she meet?"

asked Clancy.

"Now we will never find out."

Lu and Clancy headed home.

They climbed to their tree house.

"Hey! Someone has been in here," said Lu.

The keys on their desk had been moved.

There was a bite out of Clancy's donut.

Their toys had been moved.

"Who has been here?"

asked Clancy.

"Let's look for clues," said Lu.

Then they heard some cheery singing.

Clancy looked out the window.

It was Aunt Izzy.

"Come down for tea,"

she called.

"We can watch her

while we have tea," said Lu.

"I will put a burglar alarm

under the carpet," said Clancy.

"Then we will know

if anyone comes in here."

Aunt Izzy gave Lu and Clancy

lots of kisses.

"Why are you two dressed up?"

asked Aunt Izzy.

"Well …" began Lu.

Then the burglar alarm went off.

Clancy raced to the tree house.

Lu followed right behind.

"There is no one here,"

Clancy called down to Lu.

"But there are lots of footprints!"

"There are muddy footprints

down here, too," said Lu.

Lu and Clancy followed the footprints

into the house and up to the attic.

There they found Aunt Izzy,

and Sophie in a pair of muddy boots.

"I tricked you with my footprints!"

said Sophie.

"I have been teaching Sophie

some spy tricks," said Aunt Izzy.

"So you *are* a spy!" said Lu.

"Yes, I am," said Aunt Izzy.

"I will tell you all about it."

She told the pups all her spy secrets,

and where spies go for the best donuts.

Dress Up Like a Spy

You can dress up like a spy,
just like Lu and Clancy did.
Here are some tips for making
yourself look different.

1. Wear sunglasses.

2. Put a small pillow on your stomach. Use a belt
to keep it in place. Wear a big shirt or jacket to
hide the pillow.

3. A boy can wear girls' clothes. A girl can wear
boys' clothes.

4. Hide your hair under a hat.